ZELENA HOPE

We Might Hit A Planet!

Cover Art Design by Aquamarine Weasley

Cover Art Image credit to Canava.com

First edition

This book was professionally typeset on Reedsy.
Find out more at reedsy.com

To my mum, my first reader. I love you.

Acknowledgement

Thank you to my editors and beta readers. To everyone on the discord server (you know who you are!) for cheering me on with this project and supporting me when I needed it.

A huge thank you to Aqua, your cover is amazing and I love it beyond words.

Chapter 1

"It is always a very special honour to recognise the personal achievements of individual crew members as they embark on a new adventure," The General, a tall. imposing figure with closed cropped black hair and a stoop walks up and down the line of impeccably uniformed crew. I try hard not to fidget and rub my sweaty hands on the inside of my trouser pockets.

"Together, working as a team, your talents will shine," they pause, peering at us warmly. It does nothing to ease my nerves. "I'm sure that every one of you will do whatever it takes to make this mission successful."

There's a low murmur of 'Yes, General' as we haven't technically been given permission to speak.

I tap my feet as the General calls the crew forward one by one to receive awards. It's not that I don't appreciate it, but I wasn't expecting this.

"And finally," The General announces, with a twitch of their overly bushy eyebrows and with a start, I realise *I'm* the only person left in line. Oh, no. "Experience is something to be cherished. Today, we have the honour of a young man who joins with one hundred space flights, clocking in with an impressive two thousand hours!"

Alright, alright, so I may have fudged the numbers a little, but

I had to get on this ship.

The General steps forward and pins a shooting star to the lapel of my uniform. "Welcome to the family."

Heh. Family. "Thank you, General." I bow my head respectfully and step back in line.

"Now," the General clapped their hands together, "I expect you're all keen to be off," they winked at us, "so I shan't keep you too much longer. This, after all, a routine trip to Capolfen to deliver medicine. I expect you all to come home safe in eight months with tales to tell."

At long last the General dismisses us and strides away, their assistant jogging to keep up.

I head straight to the crew inspection check. It's the most tedious part of pre-boarding, and it's easier to get it out of the way first. A few of the crew that are now puffing out their chests, showing off their shiny new medals follow me towards the inspection desk. I try to remember their faces.

"Name?" The Inspector looks incredibly bored. Empty coffee cups litter the table and it's clear he'd rather be sitting down that having to stand to do this.

"Corey Arcturus Culpepper," I answer, holding my arms behind my back and trying to make this easier for the both of us.

"Rank?"

"Lance Corporal."

"Species?"

I pause, "Human."

He raises an eyebrow at my pause, narrowing his dark green eyes at me. "Planet of origin?"

"Earth."

"Where on Earth?"

"I was born under the 5th British Empire."

He squints at me, then spits on the floor. "Is that the most recent one? Earth History was never my best class."

Yes, I can tell, I think to myself. "It is."

"Age?"

"I'm 27."

"Role?"

"Maintenance Officer."

"You're on the crew manifest," I'm eventually informed, "we have assigned you cabin number 1091."

"Thank you," I say and accept the crew information sheet he gives me. Retreating away from the inspection deck, I turn my attention, at last, to the ship.

The Zenvoir, the biggest ship in the United Intergalaxy Star Fleet. It's the second most expensive ship and the newest. Despite everything, my heart beats a little faster as I gaze up at the ship. My inner child is giddy with excitement. I'm going to be a crew member on a starship, this is going to be *great*.

Chapter 2

I marked the moment the ship pulled away from space dock with a silent cheer. The maintenance team, myself included, crowded around the large windows in the Mess Hall to watch as the ship headed out into space.

Staying beside the window as the others drifted away, I let myself relax. I was here, onboard this Intergalaxy ship. There were worse ways to hitch a ride. Gazing out into the vastness of space, a sense of loneliness threated to creep up inside me. I was on my own, for the first time in decades. It wasn't something I was used to.

"Grow up," I tell my reflection in the window. My reflection stares back, weary and unimpressed. Peering closer at my reflection, I tilt my head. It's been so long, I hardly even recognise myself. Though, on the plus side, if I should blend in easier this way. Having an unremarkable face was an advantage I wished I learned earlier in life.

Shaking myself from my thoughts, I turn my back on the window and head below decks.

* * *

The maintenance staff aren't the most popular members any crew. The Captain met with us shortly after we left and clarified that we were to appear as invisible as possible. Even with all the advancements humanity has made, nothing cleans as well as a good ol' mop and bucket - even on a space ship.

We're supposed to use the maintenance shafts to get around the ship. Quietly cleaning up after the more senior members of the crew.

Family, the General had said. Yeah, right. Family treats each other with respect, and none of the maintenance team gets any of that around here. Not that I'm complaining - well, I am, a little. Being mostly ignored sits just fine with me. I'd rather not draw attention to myself. Fade into the background. That was the plan.

I should have known then. If it seems to good to be true, it usually is.

Chapter 3

"Attention, all crew is ordered to report to the Medical Deck at once."

My stomach lurches, not from the red alert siren that is blasting out, but at the idea of going to bed the med deck.

I swing my legs out of bed and hold my head in my hands for a moment. My shift ended three hours ago and I'm tired. The last thing I want to do is dress and head anywhere, but hey ho, we are but pawns to the whims of the senior officers.

Michael, my roommate (because lowly maintenance staff can't have their own cabins) runs into the room, doubled over and panting for breath.

"Slow down, what's going off?"

Before he can answer, another announcement is fighting for airspace with the red alert alarm.

"This is a reminder that crew members are to go their assigned Medical Bays on the Medical Deck."

"Gee, thanks." I roll my eyes and turn my attention back to Micheal, whose breathing has returned to normal.

"There's a rumour the away team caught something and they're dying."

"Oh," I scratch my chin, I had heard that we'd made an unscheduled stop so the Captain and his away team could go off and explore some planet or other. It had been so mundane, I hadn't paid too much attention to it.

"If they're ill and dying, why do *we* have to go up to the med deck?"

Michael can only shrug, "Who knows?"

Together we make our way slowly out of our cabin and assess the surrounding chaos. Crew members scurried back and forth, looking frazzled. Burns and rips were clear on their uniforms. A sinking feeling settled in the pit of my stomach. Whatever was going on wasn't good.

Everyone is in various states of dress and with a jolt, I realise that I'm only wearing a pair of loose light blue sleep trousers.

"Do I, do I need to put my uniform on, just head up to the med deck?" I ask wearily.

"I think you should probably put a shirt on," Michael teases.

"Yeah, fair enough."

Suitably dressed, having put on a dark blue t-shirt, Micheal and I join a group heading up the med deck, six decks above us and to our bay - bay 12. Up here, people were standing around in groups waiting to be seen by the medics.

Rumours were running rampant, and I heard several ones about who got sick and how.

The truth, when it came, was much worse than any of the rumours. The Captain, First Officer and everyone who worked on the bridge or were a part of the away team were dead. A toxic spore from a plant had gotten into the Captain's bloodstream. Anyone that had so much as a scratch was at risk from getting the toxin.

Out of a crew of close to nine hundred people, half died.

Chapter 4

"We have to turn the ship around and head back to the Space Dock!"

"We can't, we have to keep going to Capolfen!"

Lieutenants Macy Shipwright and Thomas Cline stared at each other, anger clear on both their faces.

"If I could just have your attention for the briefest of moments," The General's voice dripped with sarcasm.

The two officers looked away from each other embarrassed at the rebuke from a commanding officer.

Macy sucked in a deep breath, forcing back all tongue lashing she wanted to give to Cline. Her light green eyes flashed with annoyance. "With all due respect General, we were tasked with a mission to and we should proceed with that mission."

"I have to respectfully disagree, General," Thomas Cline interrupted, the ridges that marked him out as half Anazozian, flaring with his own fought down annoyance. The ridges started at the base of his spine and stopped at his navel.

"We've had a major health crisis and have lost every senior member of the crew. The smartest thing we can do is turn back and return to Space Dock."

On-screen, the General looked unimpressed at their behaviour. "I think the first thing that should be done is to restore order. Who is currently the most experienced person on the crew?" The General asked.

"That's alive?" Thomas asked, fake sweetly.

"T-technically," Macy began before faltering to a halt.

"That depends on how you define 'experience', General." Thomas clarifying Macy's point.

"Who on the ship has the most hours in space and has flown the most?"

Macy and Thomas glanced at each other, twin looks of horror on their faces.

"Well," Macy began helplessly sensing that the General was fast losing patience with them. "In that case, Lance Corporal Culpepper has the most experience. You yourself award him the Falling Star for over two thousand hours."

"Oh, yes!" The General brightened, cheered at this piece of news, "still around is he? Yes, he'll make a fine acting Captain."

"But General -," Thomas tried to protest.

"No buts. Culpepper will be promoted to Captain immediately, and you will obey his orders until you return to Space Dock."

"And when will that be?" Macy asked.

"That is for the new Captain to decide, isn't it?" The General grinned at them. "I'll leave it for you two to break the good news. Have him report to me as soon as knows."

The General ended the call, the screen going blank, showing the Space Fleets symbol of a galaxy on the screen.

"I'm not telling him," Thomas announced, his face sour. "They could've promoted one of us. We outrank the... *cleaner.*"

"We just need to put our trust in him."

"Trust the cleaner?" Thomas scoffed, "I'd rather not thanks."

"You don't have a choice. The General was very clear about

their orders."

"Dumbass." Thomas crossed his arms over his chest, "We're so doomed."

Chapter 5

Having two Lieutenants in my cabin was not how I expected to start my day. They weren't even naked.

"Let get this straight," I cross my legs on my bed, "*I'm* the acting Captain?"

I don't believe it. This had to be some kind of weird prank. I am not captain material. I have never been captain material. Surely these two lieutenants have lost their minds.

Lieutenant Cline is taking in my shared cabin, the clothes draped on the edge of my bed; the lack of holographic photos; the absence of any personal trinkets.

"We don't like it any more than you do," he says bluntly. "However, the General believes that with all of your experience, you're the best being for the job."

Oh right. My experience. Haha. I'm totally fucked.

"I see," I say, playing for time, "huh."

Macy moves to sit next to me, her hair pinned up in a messy updo. She looked like she hadn't slept in very many hours.

"This situation is unprecedented, none of us were prepared to suddenly be given higher ranks and responsibilities than we've been trained for."

I nod my head in agreement, even as I recall the fact that most of the ships I've been on have been kept together with duct tape and hope. There wasn't much training, it was learn on the spot with instructions or die. I suppose that's a form of training. To break the awkward silence that has fallen over us, I ask questions. "Before -," I pause, trying to think how best to word this, without saying 'before everything went to shit,' "What were you both doing?"

"I was a Cultural Advisor, with so many unique life forms on the ship, its easy for misunderstandings to occur. I'm here to smooth things over and educate where necessary."

The ridges that ran down Thomas' deep midnight black face glow a dull red, showing his annoyance, but he answers anyway, "I'm a Data Analyst," he stated firmly. "Which means that had the General used their common sense, I should've been made acting Captain."

"Ignore Thomas, I do."

"The first decisions you have to make as acting captain," Thomas pressed on, his eyes narrowed at me, "is do we proceed to Capolfen, or do we return to Space Dock?"

Oh.

Shit.

"I, well, I don't want to step on anyone's toes."

"You're the captain, it's your job to step on people's toes," Thomas' tone was drier than the Joar-Phin salt flats. "Just don't kill us all."

"What do you two think we should do?"

"I say we carry on and complete our mission," Macy stood, agitated.

"Which is the stupid thing to do," Thomas disagreed, "We should turn around and head back to Dock. We're missing half a crew, which includes all the senior officers. We *need* to return."

"We have a job to do, medicine to deliver. There are beings counting on us."

"Carrying on is stupid," Thomas snapped, "we've just had a major health crisis! We can't carry on!"

"You both have good points," I say quietly, "but I know what I want to do."

"Don't do the stupid thing," Thomas warns, voice as cold as ice.

Chapter 6

Striding onto the bridge, Thomas and Macy close behind me felt amazing. Every child, human or not, has wanted to be captain of a ship at some point. I was no different. For a second, I feel giddy with excitement. I had never been this close to the bridge before. Only the highest-ranking maintenance personnel were allowed up here.

The Zenvoir's bridge was divided into three levels. The Captain, Second Officer, and Security Advisor sat in three grand winged back chairs on the first level. Two twelve feet navigation consoles sat directly in front of the Captain's chair.

Above the Captain was the Intelligence Level, above that was the Security Level.

Walking down the steep stairs to the first level, I concentrated heavily on not falling flat on my face.

The bridge, usually a place full of activity, was empty, stripped to less than six people to run each level. On my way up here, I borrowed a crew manifest to discover who was working here currently. The last thing I wanted to do was look like I didn't know a damn thing.

I mean, I didn't know a damn thing, but the crew doesn't have to know that, do they? Exactly.

I gazed up at the faces now staring down at me. For the first time, looking up the lives that were now depending on me to make the right choice, I felt the weight of my decision pushing down on me.

Then, because my luck is so awesome, everything goes dark. There's a brief second of the light, several loud fizzing and popping noises before the ship is plunged into darkness.

"Ah," I press the comm badge of my uniform. Nothing. The lights, however, flick back on.

"Thank goodness," Macy looks worried, "the last thing we did is the power going out."

"That's what the backup generators are for," Thomas notes under his breath.

Clearing my throat, I regain the attention of the crew. "Hello," I begin, trying to project confidence into my voice. "I'm acting captain Corey Culpepper."

The crew stared down at me blankly, which really should have been my first clue that something was up.

"After much careful consideration, I have decided that we should carry on to Capolfen."

Thomas grabs me by the shoulder and swings me around. For a moment, I'm sure he's going to punch me in the face. Instead, he simply grounds out, "Are you insane?"

Spittle lands on my face, and I shudder at the feeling. Stepping away from him, I wipe my cheeks with the hem of my sleeves. "No," I say rather moodily.

"We can't just carry on you fool!"

"We can and we are," I shrug, "or do you want to tell the General that you're refusing to obey orders?"

"*Gentlemen*," Thomas and I both jump at the sharpness of Macy's tone, "please remember that you have the crew watching you."

15

Oh. Right. I knew that.

"Erm," I raise my voice and stubbornly look away from Thomas, who is standing a short distance away, arms crossed in displeasure. "I'll be reviewing everyone's records tonight and reassign people as needed. Not everyone is going to keep their current jobs. Requests will be considered."

Before Thomas can start giving me crap *again*, I turn and walk away from him, heading to the stairs and off the bridge.

Chapter 7

Sleep was impossible. After leaving the bridge, I still hadn't been able to escape Thomas and Macy. Well, more Thomas. Macy was alright.

Thomas - he - should - be - acting - captain, decided I needed to be supervised and given a tour of the ship. Even though I was, until a few hours prior, part of the maintenance crew.

Giving up on sleep, I threw off the covers and pushed myself out of bed. A part of me had expected to remain in my shared cabin with Michael. Of course, though, a captain gets his own room.

I have to say, like everything else on this ship, the captain's private cabin is pretty nice. The captain's rooms are much larger than the cabin I shared with Michael. A large bay window, reminiscent of the ones on old Earth, had a rather lovely king-sized bed tucked into it. There is nothing quite like climbing into bed underneath the stars.

On the large walnut desk, I've been scrolling through every crew member's profile on a tablet, trying to find people to fill in for the new job openings without leaving the ship too short-staffed. With half the crew dead, that had been a tall order.

Sitting in the black soft leather chair, I try to feel like a captain. With Thomas Cline breathing down my neck, it's difficult. I've read his profile. He's worked on a number of UI ships and, logically, he should have been considered for the role of acting captain.

I hate to admit it, even to my myself, but I am way out of my league here.

Shit.

* * *

I do, somehow, get some sleep. My alarm jolts me awake at 0700 hours and I roll ungracefully out of bed.

After a quick shower, it's time to face something I've been dreading.

Putting on the captain's uniform.

I've no idea who came up with these uniforms, but whoever did was high on acid.

The old maintenance crew uniform was comprised of simple dark grey trousers and matching shirt. A black lining ran around the uniforms to mark us out for the senior offices. It was subtle, classy.

I looked at the deep plum of the captain's shirt in dismay. Though I have to admit, the feel of silk on skin is much nicer than cotton. Next, I reached for the onyx black waistcoat with intricate gold lining. The final part of the over the top ridiculousness was the silk, rich black jacket. It fell to the back of my knees and had a large collar that came up to my ears and fanned out to a point. On the lapel sat the comm badge, engraved with my initials.

Four silver half-moons had been carefully had stitched onto the jackets' right shoulder, marking me out as Captain.

For more formal events, there was an added large overcoat and a half the shoulder cloak.

I tugged at the shirt collar. There was no way I was going to wear this all day. At least I could still wear my dark grey trousers!

Maybe I could get away with not wearing the jacket. Perhaps I could even get away with throwing the whole dumb uniform into an exploding star. The idea of insisting on an informal uniform while on the bridge crossed my mind, and I joyfully entertained it for a long moment. It *was* warm in the bridge and wearing this getup was going to make me melt into a puddle.

"Captain," Thomas' voice floated through the intercom. I groaned. Oh sweet Neptune, not him. "May I enter?"

No. Nope. Nah. Hard pass. Go fuck a crater, or a black hole, or a collapsing galaxy, - "Yes."

The doors were slow to open, the second sign that something may have been off.

However, with Thomas Cline swanning into the room, looking for more comfortable in his new uniform than I was completely distracted me. I had turned away from the mirror I was staring into, desperately trying to fix my hair.

As much as the man-made me want to smash his face into a control panel, he was highly skilled and well educated. I couldn't deny him a promotion. Thomas Cline was now Commander Cline, Head of Security.

Wearing a much nicer teal shirt and black trousers, Cline wore the off the shoulder cloak that I had put away and refused to look at.

"Why is your uniform nicer than mine?" I blurted out, annoyed.

Thomas fought a smirk, "I don't know, you look rather

fetching."

Oh. I coughed and looked away, glancing back into the mirror and frowning. My long reddish brown hair flowed down my back in waves. Or rather, it usually did. Today it was determined to look like a haystack.

"Thank you," I managed, remembering my manners. "I hope you like your new post."

He stood by the closed doorway for a moment, then strode confidently towards me, his movements calm and self assured.

"Here," he reached out and smoothed down my hair, "that's better."

This close, I could smell his aftershave. It made me think of running barefoot in the woods, of laughter, and warm sunny days.

"Kashiisu?" I asked.

"Oh, you know it?"

"I haven't smelled in a while," I admitted.

Thomas half smiled, "It was damn hard to find," he said, "took me six years to get hold of a bottle. I only wear it on special occasions."

"You could've just said that you like your new job," I say and take a step back. I look better. "Thank for your help," I gesture to my hair and move to stand behind my desk, putting space between myself and my new first officer.

"Why did you make Macy your new First Officer?"

"She's nice," I answer truthfully, "and you were a complete dick. I need a first officer that has my back, not one that's waiting in the wings to stab it from behind."

Thomas at least had the dignity to look abashed, "About yesterday -,"

"Forget it."

20

"No," Thomas insists, "I was mad at the General and I took that out on you. It was out of line. I'm sorry."

"That was decent of you, apology accepted." I glance at the wall clock, aware that eventually, we need to leave and face the crew. "I'm still not giving you the First Officer job."

At this, Thomas laughs, "Not yet," he winks at me.

"Let's see if everyone else likes their new roles."

"I'm sure it will be a rousing success."

"I'm sure I'll make an ass out of myself," I mutter. I fix a bright smile on my face, "Let's go!"

Chapter 8

Have you ever had to make decisions for over a hundred people that will have an effect on their lives? Did you ever have that decision blow up in your face?

Macy was sitting cross-legged in the First Officer's chair, completely at ease in her new role. At least someone was happy.

"Morning, Captain," she greeted me while a smile and stood, smoothing down her uniform that was identical to Thomas' except for the two half-moons stitched onto her right shoulder, indicting their difference in ranks.

"Morning," I nodded at her, rubbing my hands together nervously. "You look fantastic."

"As do you, Captain." Macy comes to stand on my left side, Thomas on my right. Above us, the entire bridge crew had crowded onto the intelligence level of the bridge. Some of the crew were leaning over the consoles to get a better look. Nearly all of them had frosty looks on their faces.

"Good morning everyone," I began, raising my voice so everyone could hear me. "Having spent the night going over your respective files, I have awarded you these new roles and responsibilities based on the skills you currently have. Anyone who feels disgruntled about their new job role may see me privately in my office later."

I braced myself for a wave of annoyed mutterings. Perhaps a slew of beings asking to book a time to see me.

Instead, a garbled mix of growling and what sounded like vowels reached my ears. Well, this was new.

One of the largest members of the crew, F'ck M O'tr growled the loudest. Standing at an impressive nine foot and as wide as a boar. A foot long horn jutted out from where the neck of a human would be.

"Officer Shipwright, can you translate?"

There was a long pause. "No."

"Oh," I rubbed the back of my neck. "Did anyone understand that?"

Another pause. "Erm," Thomas said, "no."

"Lieutenant commander Kiu, as head of communications, do you know..?"

Officer Kiu, who was the colour of an early morning Earth sunrise, waved her hands high in the air and gestured into the language of her people. Which, I'm sure, would've been lovely, had I known what the hell she was saying.

"I'm going to guess that the universal translator has gone down?" I say with a sigh.

Both Thomas and Macy have moved away from me, their heads bent over a navigation console.

"Captain," Macy said, voice urgent, "we're going to need to talk in private."

I run my hands through my hair, "OK, alright." Stuffing my hands into my jacket pockets. "Right, back to work everyone, Macy, Thomas, you're with me."

* * *

"How bad is it?" I ask as the office door slides shut. I peel off the jacket and waistcoat, popping open the top button of my shirt and breathing for the first time. "Fuck, I hate this uniform."

"It's pretty bad," Macy admits, taking a seat next to my desk and kicking off her heels. "I've alerted Engineering that the universal translator is down, but that's not our only problem."

"Oh, bugger."

Thomas, who until now had been standing by the doorway and tapping rapidly on a small control panel nearby, turned towards me, face grim.

"Engineering reports that the fix to the translator is going to take a while."

"Define awhile," I say, slumping into my seat behind the desk.

"A week."

"That's too long."

"Fixing the translator isn't a priority."

"Make it one," I snap, frustrated, "I need to be able to talk to the crew!"

"Captain, there are other issues that need to be dealt with first."

I lean back and cross my arms, "Is there anyone who can speak to the crew?"

Thomas and Macy look at each other, "Without learning all the languages aboard the ship - no," Macy states flatly. "Only 3% of the crew speak some kind of Earth language."

"Marvellous," I mutter. "Any more great news?"

"Most of our systems are down." Thomas paces in front of my desk.

"Great," I let my head drop onto my desk with a solid *thud*. "My first day is off to an amazing start."

I allow myself to wallow in self pity for a moment, then raise my head. "We're just going to have to overcome this," I tug at my shirt, "alright, alright, tell me everything that's broken."

"It might be easier and quicker to tell you what's working," replies Thomas dryly.

"The engines?" I ask.

"Offline."

"The food systems?"

"Offline."

"Comms?"

"Offline."

"The navigation systems?"

"Offline."

"Life support!" I ask desperately.

"Online."

"Well, at least one thing on this ship works." I fold my arms on the desk and bury my head in them.

This so very *not* good.

Chapter 9

"How long have the navigation systems been offline?"

Macy and Thomas began bickering about five minutes ago, and I've had enough. This will not to help us.

My question stops them mid argument and they both turn towards me. They look like naughty school children who have been caught by the headmaster.

"Unknown," Thomas answers after a beat, "the issue was also reported a few hours ago."

"With the crew being leaderless for so long, things have begun to get sloppy on ship. Reports aren't being filed in a timely manner, or at all. Beings aren't turning up for their shifts. I caught three beings wandering around yesterday, casually laughing that it's like being on holiday." Macy pursed her lips together tightly, affronted by the crew's new attitude.

"Before we deal with discipline or the lack thereof, we need to know where we are," I say, acknowledging Macy's point. "So, where are we?"

"We don't know," Thomas admitted, "The ship's log records us being south west of Terin, but I don't remember us passing it."

"We haven't," I drummed my fingers on the desk.

"I think it's safe to say we're lost."

"We can't be lost," I protested, "This is the second most expensive ship in the fleet and decked out with the best tech money can buy."

"Tell that to the ship's computer," Thomas huffed, "all it will tell me is that we're drifting sluggishly to port."

"You see, we're not *lost*," I say glad we're making progress, "the ship is just *drunk*."

The tension broke, Macy covered her mouth to hide her laughter while Thomas simply shook his head, the corners of his mouth tugging upwards in a smile.

"We currently have a drunk ship, a crew that has forgotten what discipline is, and nearly every important system refusing to work. Do I have that right?" I asked the pair.

Getting her laughter under control, Macy answered, "By and large, Captain."

"Hm," I looked at Thomas and Macy. This was it. If I failed to get this right, I would prove myself unworthy of leading the ship and they would rightfully report back to the General that I was unable to run a ship. They'd be right of course, I had no business running a ship.

"Thomas put a team together - take anyone from the crew that has the most knowledge of languages and find a way for all of us to talk to each other. If the Universal translator is down, then we need a viable workaround."

"Yes, Captain." Thomas bowed, inclined his head towards Macy and then strode towards the door.

I watched him leave, then turned to my attention to Macy. "We need to start getting the systems back online and for that we need Zlu."

"Agreed, Zlu is the best engineer I've ever seen on a ship."

She was close, I thought, *she's not the best*.

27

"Zlu is going to need help and I know you have a background in engineering."

Macy looked at me in surprise, "You really did do your homework." She looks around for her shoes and slips them back on.

I wanted to say that I was good at playing pretend, but I bit my tongue.

"Offer Zlu any and all help she needs. Pull crew members from other tasks. We need this ship operational and that has to be our primary concern."

"Yes, Captain."

"Don't 'yes, captain' me," I wag a finger at her, "I need you to be honest with me if I'm doing something wrong. It's your job to keep me in line."

"What are we going to do about crew discipline?" Macy asks, her lips fighting a smile.

"Throw everyone into the brig?"

"Tempting."

"I'm really not sure, lead by example I guess."

Macy nods, "Once we start dishing out orders and punishments, everyone else will fall in line. Simple. I like it."

I crack my neck and Macy winces at the sound. I grin, "Head on down to engineering then, take anyone you might need with you."

"Yes, Captain." Macy nodded, before turning on her heel and leaving.

Alone again, I hold my head in my hands. A pounding stress headache is beginning to build behind my left eye. So much for a simple trip.

With a groan, and suddenly feeling my age for the first time, I get to my feet, slip on the waistcoat and jacket, and walk towards the door.

Chapter 10

What was left of the bridge crew - F'ck M O'tr among a few others that I only recalled by sight.

The captain's chair waited for me. Imposing with its soft black leather and silver upholstery. The rightful captain had sat in that chair until his untimely death. I look away, my eyes are drawn to the large floor to ceiling screen that offered the single best view of the stars. The main bridge screen was as wide as it was long. From here, a being could stand and behold the galaxy in all its glory. It was one reason to stay as captain.

With nothing more to do, I turned and faced the captain's chair. Shaking my head, I jogged towards it and dropped into it.

On either side of the chair were panels displaying a dizzying array of buttons. None of them marked, none of them gave away what they did.

Without warning, the night blind began to lower. Clearly, someone had thought it a good idea. Well, I could stop that.

I pressed a likely looking button. It was black and just gave off a 'stop' vibe.

It was not a 'stop' button.

I, Corey Culpepper, current acting captain of the Zervoir, am never, ever pressing a button again. Not ever, not a single one. All my button pressing rights should be revoked. Someone should stand next to me, ready to slap my hand away from any buttons I may touch. Buttons are evil.

* * *

By 1300 hours, I'm covered in ash and soot. I have spent what feels like all day, the entire day, putting out fires.

I mean that in the most literal sense. After pressing that damned evil button, fires had spread all over the ship. As soon as one was put out, another started. It would've been easier to fight a hydra.

Why there is a button that starts fires like this, I have no idea. I've had no time to find out either. The crew have been scowling at me as I run past, rushing to put out yet another fire.

I feel like I've run the entire length of the ship. Twice. Sweat drips off me in rivers. Hours ago, I was forced to pin back my hair to keep it from sticking to my head.

Back on the bridge, when this madness had started, F'ck M O'tr had sucked in a deep breath and blew out - don't ask me how, I and have no idea - and had put out three fires in one go.

On every deck, reports flooded in that fires had burst into life and were causing havoc.

Macy found me on deck thirty. She had soot in her hair and on her chin. Her uniform, like mine, was slightly singed.

"What did you do?" She demanded without preamble.

"I pressed a button!"

"Captain, *please*," she tucked a loose curl behind her ear. "Be sensible."

"I am!" I huff. "I was sitting in the captain's chair and pressed a button to stop the night blind from coming down and well," I flap my arms. "It didn't stop the blind and also there's lots and lots of fire."

"Did you - did you press the slow self-destruct button?"

"Why is there a slow self- destruct button?" I ask, bewildered, "who looked at this ship and thought that was a good idea? Who even came up with the idea of a slow self-destruct and why is nothing labelled?"

"Please calm down."

"No!"

"Captain!" Macy grabs me by the shoulders and stands on her tiptoes to look me in the eye. "We can fix this."

"I've been trying!" I take a step back from her and pick up the metal bucket of water, I've been running around with this all day.

"Oh, please no."

"I've been -," as I speak, another fire begins on a nearby control panel. I douse it with water. " - throwing water -,"

" - On the control panels," Macy finishes helplessly.

"On the control panels," I confirm.

"On the *electric* control panels."

"Yes, on the - oh."

Macy Shipwright, my brand new First Officer can only stare at me in hopeless dismay. "Captain," her voice is strangled. "Please go back up to the bridge and stay there."

"No, I'm going to -," the look on Macy's face brings me to an abrupt halt. "I'm going to head back up to the bridge and stay there."

* * *

32

By the time I make it back to the bridge, the fires are thankfully out for the most part. The comms system is back online - for now, at least. Slouching across to the captain's chair, I drop into it dejected. I'm sure Macy is convincing Thomas that I can't handle the job after all. The thing is, I can't even blame her. I would be doing the same thing.

"Captain."

The comm badge on my ridiculous jacket uniform startled me out of mental grumblings.

"Yes?" I sit up straighter in my chair, cough nervously, and clear my throat. "Go ahead, Officer Shipwright."

"Zlu believes that the universal translator is going to be back online in the next half hour," she says, "I hope you haven't touched anything."

"Tell Zlu I want the translator working again in ten minutes," I say, "I haven't had time to touch anything," I add.

"Excellent," Macy sighs, "please, learn what things do, before pressing anything. I'd rather not have the ship blow up around me."

"I'm sorry. It really wasn't my attention to scare everyone like that, I'll be more careful in the future. You have my word."

"I understand, thank you, Captain. Shipwright out."

I blow out a breath and sink down in my chair. This is why I don't enjoy leading. So many people just expect you to get everything right all the time. The weight of responsibility is why I left in the first place.

I prod the comm badge, "Officer Cline."

"Captain!" Thomas' voice is getting friendlier by the hour, and I wonder if he's been drinking.

"How goes the language quest?" I ask, "I noticed you took Kiu, smart move."

33

"Thank you," I can hear him grin over the comm, "well, we started out very rocky - there were some tense moments - and then the room caught fire and now everyone is on the s'mage."

"Officer Cline, have you been drinking while on duty?"

There's a pause, then a quiet burp. "Excuse me, Captain," Thomas clears his throat. "We're all on the same page now."

"I'm glad you're all managing to work together," I say dryly, "though perhaps refrain from any more alcohol."

"Yes, Sir."

"And Cline," I lower my voice, "I don't know where you got the alcohol, but it would be decent of you to share it with your Captain."

Cline laughs, "Sure thing, Cap!"

The comm goes quiet and I shake my head. Fleet ships are *supposed* to be alcohol free. I've never believed they were, and now I have confirmation. Alcohol free indeed.

My stomach grumbles at me, reminding me I've skipped both breakfast and lunch today.

After a moment of arguing with myself - I've only been on the bridge five minutes - my stomach growls again and I give in. Food it is.

I open my mouth to tell the bridge crew that I'm heading to the mess hall and won't be long, and then I remember they aren't able to understand me. So, instead, I simply shrug and walk off the bridge.

Chapter 11

I have always found the mess hall to disappointingly small for the size of the ship it's on.

For a ship carrying hundreds of crew, the mess hall can only really comfortably hold less than a hundred beings at a time. When some of those beings are as tall as, say, F'ck M O'tr, the mess hall starts to feel very small indeed.

Ambling up to the bar, I slide onto a stool. Thankfully, no words are needed as every drink that's available is displayed in holo-form behind the bar. I point at a sea green drink that flashes up and the bartender, a telepathic being from Priviteno nods and fetches it for me. Thin as a whip and silver, beings from Priviteno are eyeless, and though they had human shaped heads, they didn't seem to use them.

The drink, a wonderful mix of Locobur and Kalais, two of my favourite fruits. Locobur is the sourest fruit you'll ever eat while Kalais is the sweetest. Kalais is banned on Earth for being so damn sweet. The two extremes come together to create a gorgeous taste explosion in my mouth. It's heavenly.

I'm just taking my second sip when the ship is plunged into darkness. The low rumble of the engines that you can hear in every part of the ship also dies away.

Oh, for the love of Neptune, what's wrong now?

I press my comm badge, "Captain to Engineering," and cross my fingers.

"Captain?" Zlu, my Head Engineer sounds shocked and relieved. "The secondary power banks are also down. We're running on emergency backup power."

"How long is that going to last?"

"Three hours, most likely less," Zlu informs me, sounding personally offended by the behaviour of the engines. "I've just sent First Officer Shipwright on her break."

"I hope she's been helpful to you," I say. Is there any way you can divert power to the mess hall doors?" I ask, there's a small crowd gathering around them, "I might be able to help."

"Even if I could, all the lifts are down. Everyone is stuck on whatever deck they happen to be on right now."

Not everyone, I muse to myself, thinking of the maintenance crew. "I have a plan, I'm going to use the maintenance shafts."

"Be careful," Zlu warns, "you'll have to manually open the maintenance doors and I can't help you."

"Don't worry," I try to reassure her, "until a few days ago, I worked in maintenance. I got this."

"In that case, I'll see you soon Captain." Zlu ends the comm call and I can tell she thinks I'm going to get stuck in a maintenance shaft. Ha, this is something I can actually do.

I make my way to the back of the mess, remembering when we were all crammed inside, watching from the windows as Space Dock became a distant speck.

So much has changed, so quickly. I push the thoughts away as I dodge around tables and crew members. It's pitch black in here, the only light coming from the weak light of the stars passing by.

My hands make contact with the smooth steel that makes up

the circular maintenance shaft hatch.

The maintenance tunnels are basically tiny ass crawl spaces. They're not made for large beings, rather they were made for beings like Zlu - slim and short - about the same size as a human toddler, come to think about it. I am not a toddler, no matter what any may say.

Using both hands and planting my feet firmly on the floor, I pull open the hatch. It opens yawns open, unused and unhappy at being opened the manual way.

I scuttle around the door and peer inside and see…nothing. The automatic lights aren't working here either. *Great.*

I press my comm badge and receive static. No comms and miles and miles of tight, dark passageways ahead of me. "Come on," I tell myself, "it's time to be useful for a change."

Chapter 12

From the mess hall to engineering are approximately sixty-eight service tunnels and forty-five ladders varying in length. All this to say, that between the tunnels and ladders there's around a thousand miles to get crawl through.

Every part of my body is pressing against something. It is not in the least bit comfortable. I'm having to crawl on my stomach just to fit. A very large part of me is hoping that this will count towards the Captain's Annual Fitness Review. The med deck has already sent me reminders that new captains have to take it post haste. No thanks, I'd rather yank my teeth out.

With almost no light and none of the systems or control panels working, I had no way of knowing if I was heading in the right direction. The only way I had to find that out was to come to the end of the shaft, leave, and find out what floor I was on.

The process was achingly slow. Coming to a junction, I had to climb *down* in the *dark. Fabulous.*

"Captain? Captain Culpepper?"

The comm dies in a rush of static before I can respond. I rest my forehead against the cool of the steel of the ladder. There is more room with the ladders, it's not enough to stop my heart from pounding and for the fear beginning to creep in. Memories from a lifetime ago threaten to resurface and overwhelm me. I may love the stars, but I loathe the dark.

"Move," I tell myself, my voice echoing loudly in the confined space. "Start moving again. Get to the engine room. Go!"

Slowly, my grip loosening off the rung, I descend once more. In the dark, I have no idea if I'm making the right decisions and heading in the right direction. As I go, I offer a quiet prayer to any Goddess that might be listening.

* * *

I'm flat on my back and gasping for breath when the Comm starts working again.

"Captain?"

Sweat drips into my eyes and I hastily brush the moisture from my brow with the back of my arm. "Yeah?" I manage, grunting as I roll over on my front. I feel as though I've lost twenty pounds in the space of - well, however long I've been doing this.

"How are you doing, Captain?" The voice sounds distant, as though trying to contact me from another ship.

My legs are shaking from the effort of having to crawl for the last few hours. I try wriggling my fingers, easing the stiffness in them. My head is pounding with pain. I want to stop and curl into a painful ball and *sleep*.

"How is the ship?" I counter, the concern is touching, but I'm expendable, the ship and the crew are not.

"The ship is holding fine," the voice sounds tense. "We -," before they can finish, the comms turns to static yet again and then goes completely silent.

I try very hard to not let this bother me. Every time the comm works, my heart leaps with joy. For a brief moment, I think, *'I'm not alone.'*

* * *

The maintenance door swings open. *'AT LAST!'* my mind screams. I have to shield my eyes from the blinding lights of the engineering room.

"There you are," the voice of Macy Shipwright sounds both pleased and exasperated, neither of which matter to me right now. Simply hearing another voice is enough to make me want to jump for joy.

"You got the lights working," I say, and raise my head, squinting to see better.

"Yes," Macy sounds as exhausted as I feel, "I'll tell you all about it, come here."

She reaches in and I clasp one of her arms. Together, I'm able to clamber out of the maintenance shaft. My legs are jelly and I fall to my knees. I want to kiss the ground. I have never been happier to be inside engineering.

"Captain?" Macy is at my side and rubbing soothing circles onto my back, "are you alright?"

"If the lights are working, please send light into the maintenance shafts," I plead.

"Oh!" Macy turns her head and finds a small looking private, "Get the lights in the maintenance shafts working, right now."

"Yes, ma'am."

Sucking in a deep breath, I push myself to my feet. "Where's Zlu? We need backup generators for the maintenance shafts.

No one should be moving around in them in the pitch dark."

"Yes, Captain," Macy replies, "I'll make a note of it."

Zlu is a tiny being. At 3ft she may be tiny, but she makes her presence known. I see her flaming red hair - the brightest, truest red you have ever seen coming full speed towards me. It looks like flowing lava. Zlu moves at 100 miles an hour.

"Lieutenant Commander," I acknowledge her with a nod of my head before she knocks me over, "how is the ship?"

"Captain?" Macy steps in as Zlu skids to a halt inches away from me, "did you - were you wearing your full uniform while in the maintenance shafts?"

I glance down at my body. I knew I was hot, but shit, I hadn't even noticed I was still in full bloody uniform.

"Fuck sake," I hiss and peel my jacket off, "Zlu, report."

"We have both generators working. Navigation and nearly all of the important computer systems have returned to full power and are running fine."

"We're making progress, that's good."

"The downside is that the engines are making signs that suggest they're going to stop working." Zlu is rocking back and forth, clearly eager to be on the move again.

"Ah well," I say, "that's where I may be helpful."

Leaving my jacket on the ground where it fell, I move towards the engines and roll up my sleeves. "I've worked on more than one cargo ship with dodgy engines," I explain as I stride over to the primary engine, a towering feat of engineering. It's bigger and thicker than anything I've worked on before, but nothing I can't handle.

"At this point, I'm willing to try anything, go right ahead." Zlu dashes off, leaving nothing but a streak of red hair in her wake.

For the first time since I became captain, I feel useful. I

know my way around an engine panel. I know how to do this blindfolded and with both my hands tied behind my back.

I call up the engine log as soon as I reach the control panels and read the information. No wonder they're fried, they've been working at full capacity since we left the dock. Not only have they not had a break, nothing on the ship has.

Working quickly, I reset the settings back to what they should have been in the first place. As soon as I do, they switch back. Someone had worked hard to override the commands. There is something very odd going on here.

My fingers fly over the control panel as I work to undo the override. I am not going to be beaten by some lousy twerp.

"Doors are operational!" Zlu calls over the din of chatter. "Universal translator back to full efficiency."

I pause, surprised. Zlu isn't human. She's from Pravoxe, the sister planet to Kafax. Zlu shouldn't have been able to speak the human Earth languages. I scrub my hands over my face. I've been awake for hours and my brain is getting sluggish if I missed that. *Wakey, wakey,* I tell myself.

"Captain!" Thomas's voice rings through the comms, clear as day. *This is more like it.*

"Officer Cline," I say, returning my attention back to the engine control panel.

"We can talk to each other," Cline informs me, jubilant. "My team and I have put together a working portable translator, just in case it ever goes down again."

"Excellent," I'm itching to know what he's done, but now isn't the time. "Whatever you've done, pass it around the crew - I want every single person to have one."

"Yes, Sir." I can hear his grin through the comm. "Cline, out."

Finally, *finally*, things are looking up.

Chapter 13

Hours later, after I've taken the main engine control panel apart along with some of the engine itself, it's done. An errant piece of computer code kept locking me out of the engines has been beaten into submission. It needs a more complete fix, but it'll keep us going for a couple of months. I'm sure Zlu is going to want to double check everything I've done.

I'm sitting on the floor, head between my knees, trying not to fall asleep. My eyes sting with tiredness, my left keeps weeping. I need sleep, but there's so much to still be done. I haven't even spoken to Cline yet about the translator workout.

As though he can hear my thoughts, Cline appears in front of me, crouching, head titled to one side as he looks at me.

"Captain?"

I look up, pushing my hair out of my eyes as I did so. "Yes, hi." I need a haircut. And sleep. Perhaps both at the same time. On second thoughts, that sounds like a bad idea.

"… this is for you," Cline finishes holding a slim black object in his hand.

I blink, I have not heard a word he's been saying. I take the object from Cline and stare at it blankly, "What is it?"

"It's the translator workaround," Cline explained, looking completely refreshed and full of energy. "You speak into one end, it translates and speaks in the correct language from the other."

"Nice," I turn over the translator in my hands, getting a proper look at it. It's sleek, for having just been made. It looks a lot like the old Earth devices from my school days. They called them mobile cells, I believe.

I want to say more, but all that escapes is a yawn, "sorry."

"How long have you been awake?"

I scratch at the stubble beginning to grow on my chin, "Since this morning. What time is it now?"

"2243, Captain."

"Oh. That's not too bad."

"It is when you've worked past your scheduled hours and isn't due to start work again until 0500 hours," Thomas says flatly. "Its time you got some sleep."

"But -,"

"No, 'buts', Captain. You can't keep going without a healthy amount of sleep and as your head of security, I'm going to have to pull rank and insist you take care of your own health for the sake of the crew and the ship."

As much as I want to disagree, my aching bones are eager to agree. I *do* need sleep. I rub at my face wearily. "Alright, you win. I'm going to head straight to my quarters," I lean back on my arms and huff out a breath, "the lifts are working, right?"

Thomas grins at me, "They are, Captain."

"Then I shall say goodnight," with a grunt I get unsteadily to my feet. "Unless there's an emergency I need to know about?"

Thomas shakes his head, "The ship is working fine," he crosses his fingers for luck. "Oh! You are wanted in the med deck once you're back on shift."

"Oh, no."

"Macy had the same reaction," Thomas seems genuinely confused, "I don't get it."

"I loathe the med deck," I say, aware I'm being grumpy and not caring. I pop my back, roll my neck and turn away from the engines for the first time in hours and begin the slow trek from the engine room to the lifts. Thomas keeps an easy stride beside me, taking one step for every two of mine. Younger, handsome, *and taller*. I want to dislike Thomas Cline, but find myself unable.

"It's not so bad," Thomas disagrees, "The medics are lovely."

I snort, "They are until they start poking you and asking questions." Bitterness laces my words and I'm unable to hide it. Thomas looks at me sharply and I curse myself for my slip.

"Well," I say, breaking the awkward silence that has fallen over us, "I'll expect to have a full report from everyone about the blackout and power failing and all of your work for 0800 hours sharp."

Thomas blanches, "I'll swap writing a report for a trip to the med deck."

"Deal."

I step into the lift, "Captain's quarters."

"Goodnight Captain."

"Goodnight."

Chapter 14

The med deck was one of the worst places hit when the illness broke out. Being so close to the outbreak, many of the medics fell ill themselves and eventually died.

Stepping onto the med deck now feels like walking into the ghost town. Even after reassigning crew members to the med deck, the place still feels empty.

"Hullo?" I peer into Med Bay 1, the Captain and First Officer's med bay and glance around. No one seems to be home. Hooray!

"Captain Culpepper," a voice says from behind me, "at last."

I turn and come face to face with my head medic, Vlaxnex Kiniz. A being I've been purposely avoiding for very nearly a week.

Vlaxnex is beautiful. Their eyes are a stunning shade of saffron with golden flecks. Their skin is a shimmering rich lavender - as though tiny galaxy are embedded into their skin the stars twinkle and move, like waves upon a shore. Like me, Vlaxnex keeps their snow white hair long - falling to the back of their knees and framing their face with expertly cut bangs.

"Lieutenant," I try to inject some warmth into my voice, "lovely to meet you, shame I have to go."

Vlaxnex isn't letting me go so quickly. They continue to stand in front of me, eyes boring into mine, making me squirm.

"I don't like being avoided."

"I don't like being here." I move to step around them - but an arm blocks my path.

"Nevertheless, as the new captain, you are due for a physical."

"I crawled halfway across the ship in maintenance shafts, I'm *fine*."

"Then why are you so afraid?"

"I'm not afraid," I fold my arms, pressing my lips tightly together to keep myself from unleashing my growing anger. Instead of fighting, I spin on my heel and march across the med bay and sit on the edge of the bed.

"Excellent," Vlaxnex hums in approval and I quietly fume. Vlaxnex takes their sweet ass time gathering medical equipment before strolling over to me, perfectly at ease.

"This isn't going to take long."

* * *

"Well?" I am done. So very done. So completely done. 'won't take long' my ass. Three hours.

Three.

Fucking.

Hours.

"I told you, I am perfectly fine!" I tug my jacket back into place with more force than necessary and hear a gentle rip. Bugger.

"I would not say perfectly, but you are, for what you are healthy."

I glare, my voice becoming cold. "I can trust that you can keep this to yourself?"

"Your medical history is private, no one else needs to know.

47

Though I have no idea why you would want to hide it."

"It's my business and I choose to *not share it*." I don't look back. I stomp out of the med bay and vow to never go back unless I have to.

Chapter 15

"Captain, it's good to see you! We have a problem."

I've taken one single, solitary step onto the bridge and already I want to turn around and leave.

"What's broken now?" I drag myself over to the Captain's chair and heave myself into it. Beside me, Macy is watching with amusement dancing in her eyes.

"You're going to love this."

"Oh no," I sink lower into the chair, chin on my chest. "Please don't let it be too bad."

"The engines have stopped." Macy drops this bombshell with the air of a mother showing off her newborn child.

"What do you mean, 'stopped'?"

"I mean, 'stopped.' As in, the engines aren't working. They have ceased to work. They have resigned. They're taking an unscheduled break," she pauses to look at me, "that kind of stopped."

"Ah," I rub at my nose, "fantastic."

"I have more exciting news."

"You know, I'm not sure I can take anymore."

"We might hit a planet."

"Hilarious," I roll my eyes, "very funny. Seriously, though, what else is wrong?"

"That wasn't a joke. Zlu reported ten minutes ago that with the engines offline, we're beginning to drift close to an Earth type planet named Triveck 32-B."

Oh shit. "I want every head of department in a meeting, right now. Call them away form whatever they're doing, even Zlu."

"Yes, Captain."

"Tell the entire crew to be on alert." I run my hands through my hair. "Blast it all to hell."

* * *

The Zenvoir along with being one of the finest ships in the fleet had the finest rooms in the fleet. The conference room was no exception.

A large heavy dark as pitch wood, known as Relany, table sits in the heart of the conference room. The genuine show stopping number, however, was the chairs the fleet had decided the use. High-backed black leather chairs, trimmed with deep gold; even the chair legs are encased in gold.

It's utterly ridiculous.

I'm kinda into it.

As I'm the first to arrive, I take out every star chart I can lay my hands on and unroll them on the table.

The maps are a much higher calibre than I'm used to. I know a good few captains that would *kill* to get their hands on these. I know some who have. These maps have the ability to switch from a 2D object to a 3D moving holographic, depending on what you need it for. I switch it to the holographic and narrow in on Triveck 32-B.

We're dangerously close to the planet's atmosphere. I'd give it a few hours before the ship beings to lean to starboard and gets pulled into the atmosphere and causes us to crash into the planet. 160 million beings. The entire crew of the Zenvoir - all dead.

"Captain," Thomas strides confidently into the room, still wearing his uniform as though it was made perfectly for him. "Good morning."

"What's good about it?" I ask, closing down the holographic and rolling up the maps. "Where's Zlu?"

"On her way at a guess," Thomas drops into a chair, placing his feet on the table, "you doing OK?"

"YE-no," I slump into my chair, head held into my hands. "I apologise for being so testy."

"You know," Thomas says thoughtfully, "when you were made Captain, I was really, really, pissed off."

"I remember."

"I didn't think you can handle it and yet, here we are. You've done so much for this crew, for this ship. I trust you."

I raise my head, stunned at Thomas' words. "I -, thank you."

For a moment, our eyes lock across the table. His warm russet brown eyes change into a liquid black as time stops still.

I look away first, aware of everything I'm risking if I let this silly crush grow into anything more.

Luckily, I'm distracted from my thoughts with the arrival of all the senior officers.

Macy makes a beeline straight for me and kicks her heels off before sinking into the chair next to mine.

"You should really stop wearing those if you hate them so much," I tease. Macy snorts.

"Are you kidding? They make my legs look great."

"Mmm, that they do."

Macy flashes me a grin as around us, everyone settles down into their seats. I risk a look at Thomas, to find him deep in conversation with Ylux Xioklio, older sibling to Zlu, and my Chief Science Officer. Thomas has a deep set frown between his eyes as he listens to Ylux speak. He notices me watching and winks.

"Cute, isn't he?" Macy whispers, leaning against me with a knowing smile. "You should see him naked."

I'm not quick enough to hide my surprise, and I'm rewarded with Macy's laugh. To cover my awkwardness, I stand up and clear my throat. Twelve sets of eyes gaze at me expectedly.

I take a fortifying breath and begin.

Chapter 16

"You're saying our best plan is what?" I'm standing, hands pressed onto the table, staring that the holographic as Zlu manipulates the graphic to make Triveck 32-B larger.

"If we fail to restart the engines, then we're going to have to force the ship to somehow fall port side."

Triveck, its orange waters shining on all our faces, rotates slowly in front of my eyes.

"Have we managed to make contact with the planet?"

"Still trying to reach them, Captain," Kiu speaks softly, her voice a light musical lilt. "I'll keep trying."

"Good," I feel completely frustrated. There is no question that Triveck needs to be warned of the impending danger, and yet there is only so much I can do and a clock ticking down to disaster.

"Zlu, a private word."

I walk to the back of the conference room, Zlu close behind. As I walk, I plan out what I want to say, without sounding paranoid.

"I don't want to alarm you," I lower my voice, "but there is something wrong with this ship."

To my surprise, Zlu nods, her red hair shimmering in the starlight from the windows. "You mean, like, how there seems to be a code built into the ship's primary engine? One that keeps threatening the safety of the ship?"

"Has this happened since the blackout?"

"Twice," Zlu sounds angry, and I can't blame her. "Both times I noticed before anything serious could happen." She looks away, "Captain, I feel as though this is partly my fault. I should have kept a better eye on it and -,"

"It's not your fault," I cut her off and try to sound reassuring. "You can't be everywhere at once. The fact you stopped this twice already is commendable."

"Thank you, Captain." Zlu stands stiffly beside me, unused to being so still.

"You can call me Corey, or Culpepper - there's no need to be so formal around me." Please, *please* don't be so formal, I silently beg.

"Captain," Zlu responds after a moment, "I don't think I can stop this - bug - the code from attacking the ship."

* * *

"Thomas!" I catch his arm as the meeting ends, "I know things have been hectic, but I wanted an update on how the security team is going." After the blackout, I woke up in the middle of the night with the sudden knowledge that I hadn't given Thomas a security team.

"Pretty well," Thomas ruffles his perfect hair, "I should have everyone finalised soon."

"Excellent." We fall into step as we walk out onto the bridge. Macy smirks at us.

"I feel like I'm missing something," Thomas looks between

Macy and myself, "what has she said?"

"Nothing I'd like to repeat," I admit, speeding up my walk to hide the blush creeping up my cheeks.

"Adorable," Macy croons sweetly.

I roll my eyes, "An update Officer Kiu?"

"We managed to make contact briefly, however, our communications array has stopped working. I've filed a report with Lieutenant Commander Zlu."

Right, I've had enough. "Officer Shipwright, I'm going down to the engine room to assist Zlu, if anything happens - we go back into another blackout or the comms go down, anything, I want you to take over command of the ship."

"Captain - are you sure?"

"Very sure," I say, turning to look at Thomas. "Officer Cline, time to put your new security team to the test. I want groups of two guarding the entrance to the bridge and the engine room."

"Right away, Captain."

"Corey," Macy places a hand on my arm, "what's going on?"

My breath ghosts against her pale skin as I whisper into her ear, "someone is attempting to sabotage this ship."

Chapter 17

"Officer Zlu to Captain Culpepper," I'm between floors in the lift, on my way to engineering when Zlu comms me. My heart sinks.

"Culpepper here."

"Triveck 32-B is readying their weapons. They're going to fire on the ship."

Oh shit. *Shit. Shit. Shit.*

"Thank you, for the warning," I say, stunned into near speechlessness. I tap my comm badge, licking dry lips.

"Captain Culpeper to all personnel, prepare for an incoming attack. Please proceed to red alert and stay on guard. Captain out."

"Officer Cline to Captain Culpepper."

"Go ahead, Cline."

"Captain, should we ready the weapons to fire back?"

"No!" Ice grips my heart. "Do not return fire."

"Yes, Captain," Cline sounds relieved. "I'm redirecting all non-essential power to the shields."

"Fantastic. Do whatever you need to do to make sure the ship is safe, that's an order."

"Understood."

Less than a minute later, the ship shakes as the first missile hits the shield.

They seem to hold, which is honestly kind of a surprise and a relief with this ship and how things have been going lately.

Two more missiles strike as I walk through the door of the engine room. Smoke billows out, as dark and as thick as tar. I cough and pull my jacket around my mouth.

As I walk deeper into the room, I find Zlu - visible only because of the molten red hair that weaves through the smoke as she bustles about. All around her is chaos, and yet Zlu seems utterly at ease.

I spot a private passing by and stop them. "Report, Private."

"Er," they look around, their eyes darting everywhere as they wring their hands, shaking with nerves. "I-I think some people were injured."

"It's going to be OK," my tone softens, "What's your name?"

"Revel McKenna," light green eyes find my jacket and the three half-moons. "Oh! Captain!"

"Has anyone died?" I ask gently, not wanting to startle them further.

"No, at least, I haven't seen -,"

"Thank you for your help, Private McKenna," I squeeze their arm in what I hope is a reassuring way and press on, into the smoke and chaos.

"ZLU!" I call over the smoke, "ZLU!"

"Captain!" Zlu is wearing a mask and has several more dangling from her hands. She thrusts one at me. "Put this on."

The masks filter and regulate clean air for up to an hour.

Slipping the mask on, I feel better instantly. "What's happened?"

"One of the missiles dislodged a valve inside the primary

57

engine and the ventilators are down." For the first time, I see fear cross Zlu's face.

"Captain, if we don't get help soon, we're going to have to evacuate the ship."

"Show me the engine," I say. Entering the primary engine can only be done by trained professionals - and both of ours died because of the illness. For as talented as Zlu is, she's not trained to go into the engine itself. For that matter, neither am I - but that's never stopped me before.

Zlu leads me towards the engine and the smoke becomes thicker and denser with every step.

By the time we reach the engine - which in normal circumstances would take a minute or two - has taken nearly ten, our masks are struggling. The smoke is so thick, I could write my name in it.

The door into the engine is now leaning to one side, blocking any entry. Some of the glass has broken, which explains why the smoke is so thick.

My eyes water from the smoke as I take in the damage. Ideally, we'd turn back to Space Dock and get repaired, but with navigation down and being way off course, turning around is not an option.

There is only one thing I can do that has a shot of working. I rake my hands through my hair. Bugger. I didn't want to have to do this, but I'm being backed into a corner. If the ship is going to survive and not crash into Triveck 32-B, I need to do this.

I head back to where the air is more breathable and turn to face Zlu, who has been following close behind, hands on hips, waiting.

"I have a plan, but it's risky," I state matter-of-factly. "This

58

is what I need you to do - clear everyone out of here. No, I'm serious. Get everyone out. If this goes wrong, anyone still close to the engines is going to be hurt. If this works, I need you to throw the engines into reverse and get the hell away from Triveck. Tell Officer Shipwright that I want everyone on evacuation standby."

"What are you doing?" Zlu asks baffled, "No one can get into the engines, no one -,"

"Zlu," I plead, "trust me."

"If you're in danger, get out," Zlu says after a long moment and then breezes past me, firing off orders to the engine crew.

Shrugging out of my uniform jacket - really, this uniform is utterly over the top - I make my way back towards the engines. I peel off my waistcoat and shirt, then shuck off my shoes. If I'm going to do this, there is no point ruining good clothes - even if they are dumb.

The engine stands before me, a giant glass cylinder that encases twenty 30 foot pistons. Four more cylinders form a ring around this, the main one.

Walking past the broken door, I stand close to the glass. This close and I still can't see the damaged valve.

Gritting my teeth, I push my hand through the glass. Pain shoots up my arm and sweat breaks out on my forehead.

The process is slow and wracks my entire body with pain. First one arm. Then a shoulder.

Eventually, I manage to pull myself through the glass. Heat and smoke beat themselves upon me, filling up my senses. My head swims with exhaustion. Only the thought of finding and fixing the valve keeps me going.

Chapter 18

"The Captain is gone."

The words echo around Macy's brain as she tries to fathom what they mean. How can he be gone? It doesn't make sense.

"Gone?" she echoes, bewildered.

She and Thomas are standing beside the captain's office on the bridge.

Thomas fell silent as soon as Zlu broke the news over the comm, falling against the wall. His face slack with surprise.

Fuck, is Macy's first thought. *Damn this ship just eats up its captains*, is her second.

They feel inappropriate.

"What happened?" Macy asks, throat tight.

"I'm not sure," Zlu sniffs, it's clear she's been crying. "He ordered everyone out of the engine room. I went to see what he was doing and he - he -,"

There's a long pause as Zlu tries to collect her thoughts. "He walked into the primary engine."

"Oh." Macy tries to imagine anyone walking into the primary engine and fails. It's not possible. No one - human or otherwise could pass through solid glass.

Thomas snorts, pushing himself away from the wall and stalks off. Macy watches him go.

"Thank you for letting me know Zlu." She taps her comms badge, ending the call.

Another captain lost. How in the universe was she going to break the news to the crew?

Pressing the comm badge again, she chews on her bottom lip. "Zlu, are the engines working?"

Macy stares out of the bridge screen, Triveck looks incredibly *too close*.

"Two minutes until full power is restored," Zlu screams, elated. "He did it! He fixed the engines before -, well, he saved us."

Macy ends the comm call, blinking back tears of gratitude.

"Prepare to reverse at full speed," she informs the navigation team. "Then take us the hell away from Triveck."

"Yes, Captain." Corporal Lowe, a messy haired blonde, turns to look at her and winks.

"Until we have proof Captain Shipwright is de- no longer with us, it's *First Officer*, Lowe."

Lowe rolls his eyes, turning his attention back to the navigation panel in front of him. "Whatever you say, ma'am."

Chapter 19

Inside, the engine space is cramped. I have to wiggle and crawl to get anywhere. Time has no meaning here, it's worse than having to crawl through the maintenance shafts. At least I don't feel like my skin is coming off when I'm doing that. Toxic fumes wrap around my body like a lover, making it harder and harder to breathe. With every pull of my lungs, I feel close to the edge of passing out.

* * *

I have no idea if I was able to fix the engine in time. No idea if the ship was saved. I'm drained through having to do this. All I know for sure is that I ache deep in my bones and that in my hands, I'm holding the reason the engines were so messed up in the first place.

I stagger out, wave at a teary looking Zlu, offering her a weak, bright smile, and then all is dark as I promptly pass out.

About the Author

Zelena Hope lives in England with her cat Shadow, where she spends most of her time crying over comma splices.

Website under contruction.

You can connect with me on:
🐦 https://twitter.com/ZelenaHope
📘 https://www.facebook.com/Zelena-Hope-113225110083646

Subscribe to my newsletter:
✉ https://sendfox.com/zelenahope

Printed in Great Britain
by Amazon